WITH SPECIAL THANKS TO LINDA CHAPMAN

First published in Great Britain in 2013 by Simon and Schuster UK Ltd
A CBS COMPANY

Text Copyright © Hothouse Fiction Limited 2013
Illustrations copyright © Mary Hall 2013
Designed by Amy Cooper

1 3 5 7 9 10 8 6 4 2

Simon & Schuster UK Ltd
1st Floor, 222 Gray's Inn Road
London
WC1X 8HB

Simon & Schuster Australia, Sydney

Simon & Schuster India, New Delhi

A CIP catalogue record for this book is available from the British Library.

PB ISBN: 978-0-85707-254-2
eBook ISBN: 978-0-85707-697-7

Printed and bound by CPI Group (UK) Ltd, Croydon, CR0 4YY
www.simonandschuster.co.uk
www.simonandschuster.com.au
www.spellsisters.co.uk

AMBER CASTLE

CHLOE
THE STORM SISTER

Illustrations by Mary Hall

SIMON & SCHUSTER

Silver Hill

Croxton Manor

Morgana's Lair

Avalon

St. Stephen's Church

Fairview Vineyard

Woolston Manor

Sunnyvale

Clement Castle

Halston Castle

Glendale Stables

Belleview
Bridge

N

Spell
Sisters

Deep in the woods . . .

The rays of the setting sun fell on the water, making the Lake glitter. A ring of tall trees surrounded it, their bare branches reaching up into the sky as if asking for help. Morgana Le Fay stood in the shadows of the forest. Her eyes were black as coal in her pale face, and the hem of her long dark dress touched the fallen leaves that carpeted the ground. She was staring at the mist-covered island in the centre of the Lake like a hawk watching its prey.

'*Soon*,' she muttered greedily. 'Soon Avalon and all its power shall be mine, and then nobody will be able to stop me.'

A cruel smile pulled at Morgana's mouth as she thought of the magic she would work when she was finally free to take over Avalon. The island had great power, and she intended to harness it and use it for her own dark purposes. Everyone in the kingdom would know her name and fear her. It *would* happen – she would not be stopped. Eight Spell Sisters usually lived on the island to protect it from harm using their magic, but Morgana had captured all of the sisters and trapped them away from the island. Seven of the sisters had managed to escape and return to the island, but she still had one of the sisters of Avalon in her power. And with even just one Spell Sister under her spell, the others were weak enough for her to triumph over them.

'The eighth sister will *never* be free. I *shall* claim Avalon!' she hissed.

But as she spoke, a picture of two girls filled her head – a tall girl with chestnut hair and a determined look in her green eyes, and a small, pretty blonde girl with eyes as blue as cornflowers.

Morgana frowned. No – those two girls might have been the ones to free seven of the Spell Sisters, but they would not stop her this time. She lifted her chin and strode out of the trees towards the Lake. She stepped on to the black rocks that surrounded the shining water and the mirror-like surface instantly rippled and a beautiful lady rose up through the water. The lady stood magically on the surface, staring at Morgana with fierce, dark eyes.

'Stop!' she commanded, her voice ringing out. 'You shall not cross to Avalon, Morgana! You know I have put a strong spell of protection on the Lake. You cannot reach the island.'

'Your spell will only last for one more day, Nineve.' Morgana Le Fay looked triumphantly at the Lady of the Lake. 'Tonight, finally, is the night of the lunar eclipse. When the moon is covered by shadows, your magic will break and I will be waiting here. I *shall* cross to the island at last!'

A look of worry crossed Nineve's face but she hid it quickly. 'My spell might fade, but we will defeat you!' she cried.

Morgana laughed harshly. 'Don't be foolish. We both know I shall win. Unless all eight Spell Sisters are on the island tonight, Avalon will be mine, and I still have one sister under my spell! ' Her eyes flashed at the thought of victory and she shot one hand into the sky.

Dark storm clouds formed above the Lake and passed over it, as if blown by an invisible wind. The clouds met and suddenly rain started to pour down, hitting the leafless branches of the winter trees on the island and splashing down around Nineve as she stood on the Lake's surface. Meanwhile, the space immediately around Morgana stayed dry. She clicked her fingers and the rain turned to vicious hailstones. Nineve cried out and shielded her face as the frozen droplets battered into her.

Morgana laughed again cruelly. 'This is just a taste of what I can do! Tonight, as your spell of protection fades, you shall feel the full force of my power.'

The hailstones increased and Nineve took refuge in the water, sinking quickly beneath the surface of the Lake.

Morgana clapped her hands. Lightning forked through the sky, hitting one of the trees on the far side of the Lake. It burst into flames, sending sparks flying up into the air and over the Lake.

Morgana raised both her hands. 'Yes, tonight Avalon shall at last be mine!' she screamed into the storm clouds. *'Mine!'*

1

Wedding Bells

'D o stand still, Guinevere!' Lady Matilda said sharply. 'How can Meg possibly fit your bridesmaid dress if you squirm like that?'

'I'm sorry, Aunt Matilda.' Gwen swallowed and tried to stand still while Meg, the dressmaker, knelt beside her, pinning up the pale blue dress. But it was so hard not to fidget. Gwen hated being still, and right now it was more difficult than ever. There was so much she wanted to be doing!

She looked out of the castle window. She could see the forest beyond the castle grounds. Frustration buzzed through her like a bluebottle trapped in a jar. She wanted to be out there. Her fingers touched the blue pendant she wore around her neck, which had been given to her by Nineve, the beautiful Lady of the Lake.

Gwen and her cousin, Flora, had first met Nineve when they had gone for a walk and found the pendant on a silver chain stuck in a rock by the magical Lake in the centre of the forest. Gwen had managed to pull the pendant and chain out of the solid stone, then the water parted and Nineve had appeared. Gwen knew she would never forget that moment.

Nineve had told them that the evil sorceress Morgana Le Fay had captured the eight Spell Sisters who lived on Avalon and trapped them because she wanted to take the magical island as her own. Nineve had cast a spell to prevent Morgana from crossing the Lake, until she could find a way to rescue all the Spell Sisters.

Nineve had gone on to explain that the stars foretold that the person who could pull the pendant from the stone would be able to help save Avalon and the kingdom. And it seemed she was right! So far, Gwen and Flora had managed to free seven of the Spell Sisters – but the eighth sister was still trapped somewhere. They had to rescue her before the lunar eclipse when Nineve's spell would fade. But time was really running out, the eclipse was due to take place that very evening!

Gwen longed to run to the Lake to talk to Nineve. But preparations were underway for a grand wedding at the castle the next morning and sneaking off unnoticed was proving difficult. She and Flora were bridesmaids, and they were supposed to be taking part in a rehearsal for the wedding that afternoon.

Weddings! Gwen huffed inwardly. Most young noble girls couldn't wait to get married, but she really couldn't understand why anyone would want that. Gwen wanted to travel and have adventures. She liked riding and shooting with her bow and arrow. She didn't want to have to stay at home, run a household and do what a husband told her to do.

Just then Flora came into the room. She had already had her bridesmaid fitting and was back in her day clothes – a pretty yellow dress with a gold sash around the waist and golden ribbons woven into her blonde plaits.

'Ah, there you are, Flora,' Lady Matilda said. 'Is it almost time for the wedding rehearsal?'

'Yes, mother,' Flora replied. 'I've just been speaking to Cousin Bethany, and she was wondering if Gwen was ready yet.'

'We shall be finished any moment,' said Lady Matilda.

Meg put in the last pin and straightened up. 'All done, your ladyship.'

'Very good, Meg. Gwen you may change

back into your everyday clothes and then go with Flora to the chapel. I will see you both there.'

'Yes, Aunt Matilda,' Gwen murmured, bobbing a curtsey.

Lady Matilda swept out of the room. Gwen quickly changed back into her comfy green dress with its leather belt while Meg took the bridesmaid dress away for alteration.

'This wedding is going to be so much fun!' said Flora.

'Fun?' Gwen exclaimed, tugging up her long sleeves. 'How can we possibly have fun when the final Spell Sister is still trapped?'

Flora's face fell and instantly looked guilty.

Gwen sighed, but forgave her cousin. She knew that Flora really loved things like wedding and feasts and jousting tournaments. But this was really important. 'What are we going to do?'

Gwen said. 'We have to rescue the last sister by tonight or Morgana's evil plan will succeed.'

Flora nodded, looking serious now. 'I know. The pendant hasn't glowed at all today, has it?'

'No,' Gwen replied. Previously, when Nineve wanted to get in touch with the girls, she had made Gwen's pendant shine and then her image would magically appear in the jewel's surface. But they hadn't heard anything from the Lady in the Lake for several days now though.

Flora sighed. 'There's not much we can do about it now, we have to get to the chapel now for the rehearsal or Mother will be cross.'

Gwen knew Flora was right. They simply couldn't risk annoying Lady Matilda, if they did, she was likely to confine them to their bedchamber and then they'd have no chance of slipping away at all. Gwen took one last look out at the forest through the arched window. *Oh, Nineve, please find out where the sister is trapped,* she thought. *Let us know in time to help.*

'All right,' she said, turning to Flora. 'Let's go.'

'You'd better brush your hair first,' said Flora, looking at Gwen's tangle of reddish-brown curls and shaking her own head. 'Mother won't be impressed if you turn up looking like a bird has been nesting in your hair, and we should do everything we can to keep her pleased with us while there's a sister to save.'

Gwen rolled her eyes, but picked up a hairbrush from the side and tugged it through her thick hair. 'Better?' she said, after a few minutes.

'Well . . . ' said Flora, considering it, 'you could always braid it and put a ribbon in it? It would make it look much neater.' She picked up a ribbon from the side.

'No, no,' Gwen said backing off. She couldn't see the point of decorating her hair with ribbons and headbands. 'It's fine as it is!'

Flora smiled a little. She knew her cousin all too well. 'All right, suit yourself. It's tidy enough for Mother. Let's go.'

The girls put on their outdoor cloaks and leather boots, and then headed out of the castle. Their cousin, Bethany, was getting married in a small chapel in the forest. It was a little grey stone building standing in a small clearing, surrounded by trees. Its windows were made of stained glass showing pictures of pilgrimages and fables from long ago.

When Gwen and Flora arrived, they found most of the castle household milling around. There was Aunt Matilda and Uncle Richard,

along with Gareth the squire and the six young pages who lived at the castle and were training to be knights. Thomas the priest was there, as he was going to be conducting the ceremony, and there were also the minstrels who were going to be playing music at the wedding. Bethany was talking to her husband-to-be, a young knight called Guy le Marquand.

'Oh, I still think weddings are sort of silly,' Gwen murmured to Flora.

'They're not! Look at Guy. Isn't he handsome?' sighed Flora, her face dreamy as she looked at the bridegroom. 'Bethany's so lucky.'

Gwen rolled her eyes. 'Lucky? Guy's eyes look like a bullfrog's and his ears are as big as Old Spot the pig's. In fact, I'd sooner marry Old Spot than marry him!'

Unfortunately her words were overheard

by Will, the most annoying of the pages. 'What? Gwen wants to marry a pig!' he whooped. 'Did you hear that everyone? *Oink! Oink!* She wants to marry Old Spot!' He did a pig impression that made the watching pages laugh. 'Well, I doubt even Old Spot would want to marry you, Gwen— WHAA!' He broke off with a yell as a tall, blond page casually stuck out his foot and Will tumbled over, landing in a pile of fallen leaves.

'Arthur!' Will yelled furiously as he sat up with leaves now stuck in his hair.

'Oh, sorry,' said Arthur, looking anything but. 'I don't know what happened there. You just seemed to walk into my foot. How strange!'

Will glared at him, but although he was older than Arthur, the younger boy was just as tall and strong as him. Will clearly didn't want to start a fight he might lose with people watching so he stomped off, muttering to himself.

Gwen turned to Arthur and grinned. 'Thank you!'

'Any time,' he said, giving her a slight bow. 'So you don't like weddings then?'

'Not really,' said Gwen with a shrug. 'They're dull. I'd much rather be out in the woods shooting with my bow and arrow.'

'Me too,' Arthur said. 'We should go out and have an archery contest together again some time. We haven't done that for ages.'

Gwen nodded. She liked that idea – and she liked Arthur. He never treated her like she was just a girl.

'You always seem to be so busy at the moment,' he said to her. 'Where do you and Flora keep going off to?'

'Nowhere special,' said Gwen hastily. 'Just,

um, different places.' *That was certainly true,* she thought. They'd been to an old vineyard, an abandoned castle, a cave in the forest . . .

'Positions please, everyone!' called Thomas the priest, clapping his hands. 'Ushers and bridegroom into the chapel, bride and bridesmaids by the outer door!'

Flora and Gwen hurried to line up behind Bethany outside. Flora nudged Gwen as they took their places a few paces back from the bride. 'So, would you still think a wedding was stupid if it was you getting married to Arthur?' she teased.

Gwen blushed. 'Don't be silly, Flora!'

'I saw you talking to him,' Flora whispered with a giggle. 'Maybe you'll end up getting married to him one day.'

Gwen blush deepened. 'I told you, I'm never getting married if I can help it,' she hissed.

'Mmm.' Flora's blue eyes twinkled. 'You and Arthur, I can see it now . . . '

Bethany looked round and shushed them sharply. 'Girls – please!'

Flora finally stopped her teasing, and the music started inside the chapel. Bethany walked in though the door, and with a sigh Gwen took one last longing look at the forest and followed her inside.

Keeping Secrets

It was cold inside the little chapel as they stood and listened to Bethany and Guy practise saying their vows. Gwen was already starting to feel a bit bored as she stood behind Bethany, and she glanced around idly at the decorative windows of the little church. Most of the stained glass panes were old and dusty, so she couldn't really see through them out to the forest. Wishing she could be outside again, Gwen watched little circles of sunlight dancing on the floor, shining in through what seemed to be a newer, cleaner window. As Gwen watched the spots of light, she thought about Avalon and the way the light danced on the Lake around it.

Where could the last Spell Sister be trapped, and what exactly were her powers? Each of the sisters of Avalon had a magical power that related to nature and elements and Nineve had told them that the eighth sister was Chloe the Storm Sister, so Gwen guessed that must mean she had power over the weather. Morgana had been able to use the magic of each of the Spell Sisters while they were trapped and with all the other sisters now safe, the only power Morgana could use, apart from her own magic, would be

Chloe's. *I really hope we find Chloe in time*, Gwen thought anxiously, she didn't like to think what would happen if they failed.

At long last the rehearsal came to an end. 'Well done everyone, our practise is done,' announced Thomas. 'You may all now return to the castle. I'll see you all tomorrow for the happy event!' he finished with a smile.

Gwen breathed a sigh of relief. With the rehearsal now over everything was ready for the wedding. Maybe *now* she and Flora could finally slip away.

'Gwen? What's *that?*' She looked round to see Arthur staring at her dress. Gwen glanced down to follow his gaze and gave a squeak of alarm. The blue pendant, tucked inside the neck of her dress, was glowing!

Arthur blinked at the shining light.

'What . . . what is it?'

'Nothing!' Gwen hastily pulled her cloak around herself, hiding the light. 'Nothing at all!'

'But there's something shining around your neck...'

Explanations tumbled through Gwen's head, but she knew Arthur was too clever to be fobbed

off with a lie. There was only one thing for it –
to tell him the truth. Or at least a little bit of it.
'Please, Arthur,' she begged quietly, checking to
see no one else was listening. 'Don't say anything
to anyone. You're right, my necklace is glowing.'

'Is it . . . magic?' he whispered in awe.

She hesitated for a moment, and then
nodded. 'I wish I could tell you all about it,
I really do but I can't. I've promised not to tell
a soul. Flora is the only other person who knows
what's going on.'

His eyes met hers. 'All right,' he sighed. 'If
it's a secret I won't ask any more. You mustn't
break a promise.'

Gwen could have hugged him. 'Thank you!'
she said, reaching over to squeeze Arthur's arm
gratefully. 'Now, I need to talk to Flora, but we
can't have anyone else notice us slip away . . . '

Gwen glanced over at Flora, who was standing with the pages by the chapel door.

'I'll distract the others for you,' said Arthur.

Gwen grinned widely. 'That would be really helpful, thanks.'

Arthur strode to the door. 'Hey, who wants a wrestling contest? Bet I can beat the lot of you with one hand tied behind my back!'

There was an immediate outcry from the other pages.

'No you can't—!'

'You're talking a load of pigswill—'

'You'll *certainly* never beat me!' Will interrupted with a sneer.

'Well, I suppose there's only one way to find out,' said Arthur. 'Race you to the keep!' He set off and, fired up by the challenge, the other pages chased after him like a pack of hounds hunting a hare.

'So,' Flora came over to her, her eyebrows raised. 'You and Arthur looked like you were having a cosy chat?'

'Flora, there isn't time for this now!' Gwen whispered. 'The pendant's glowing!'

The teasing look dropped instantly from Flora's face. 'Glowing? That means Nineve must be sending us a message!'

Gwen nodded. 'We need to find somewhere private so we can find out what she's needs to tell us.'

She darted out of the chapel with Flora following. The pages had disappeared back towards the castle, and only a few adults remained, talking as they made their way back as well. 'This way,' said Gwen, quickly leading the way into the trees near the chapel.

They hid behind the wide trunk of a horse chestnut tree and Gwen pulled out the pendant. As well as the pendant, seven gems hung on the silver chain. Each one had been given to Gwen by a different sister of Avalon to say thank for rescuing her. There was a fire agate stone from Sophia, an emerald from Lily, a piece of amber from Isabella, a purple amethyst from Amelia, a sapphire from Grace, a ruby from Olivia and a pearl from Evie. The blue pendant Gwen had originally pulled from the stone by the Lake was larger than all of them. It was now sparkling with light.

'Nineve?' Gwen whispered, picking it up.

A mist swirled across the pendant's surface

and an image of the Lady of the Lake appeared in it. She had dark eyes and long chestnut hair, and she wore a shimmering green and blue dress that fell to her ankles. A circle of pearls held back her thick hair from her beautiful face. 'Guinevere! Flora!' she said. 'You must come to the Lake with all speed!'

'Now?' Gwen said.

'Yes. I have finally found out where Chloe, the eighth sister, is trapped.'

Gwen and Flora exchanged excited looks.

'You must rescue her before tonight,' Nineve went on, her eyes full of intent. 'My protection spell will fade as soon as the lunar eclipse starts. As the Earth, moon and sun move into line, a shadow will cross the moon and when it falls completely dark, the spell will break and Morgana will be able to cross the Lake and reach Avalon.' Nineve hesitated, and her voice wavered a little. 'Once she is there, nothing will stop her from using its power to bring chaos to the kingdom. Our only chance is to free Chloe the Storm Sister so she can join with her sisters on Avalon. Together, the eight Spell Sisters have enough power to keep her from reaching the island.'

'We'll come to the Lake straight away.' Gwen said.

'Thank you, girls. I will see you soon.' Nineve said.

The image in the pendant faded.

'The last Spell Sister, finally,' said Flora. She looked excited but nervous. 'I wonder where she's trapped?'

'I don't know,' Gwen said anxiously. 'We need to find Moonlight. He'll be able to take us to the Lake as quickly as possible. There's no time to lose.' She walked further into the trees and whistled softly. Moonlight was a wild white stallion. The girls had found him in the woods on their first adventure, and Gwen had fed him an apple from Avalon. After eating it, he had developed magical powers – he could gallop at incredible speed, and seemed able to understand the girls. He lived in the woods, but Moonlight was always there for them when they needed him.

Gwen listened for a moment, and then whistled again. This time, while the sound of Gwen's summons was still echoing through the trees, there was the soft thud of hoofbeats, and then Moonlight came trotting through the trees. His ears were pricked and his neck arched proudly. His mane and tail hung in soft silky strands and his coat was the colour of freshly fallen snow.

Gwen's heart leapt as it always did when she saw him. She smiled, and hugged his neck quickly. 'We need to go to the Lake, Moonlight. Please can you take us there?'

The stallion whickered and walked over to a fallen tree trunk. He stood there patiently, as if telling the girls to use it to get on his back. Gwen helped Flora on and then vaulted up behind her cousin. The stallion's back was warm and soft.

Flora wrapped her hands in his mane. 'Oh please, Moonlight,' she breathed. 'Take us to the Lake as fast as you can.'

Moonlight plunged forwards. He swerved round, in and out of the trees, but his special Avalon magic meant that the girls were never in danger of falling off.

'We'll be there in no time!' Gwen cried to

Flora, as she held on tight around her cousin's waist. But just then Moonlight skidded to a sudden halt, leaves and mud flying up from under his hooves as a figure stepped out unexpectedly from the trees.

It was a man with a long grey beard. He was wearing a dark green hooded cloak and holding a wooden staff. His weathered face was wrinkled with age.

'Greetings my friends!' he said in a deep, booming voice.

Gwen blinked as she recognised the old man. 'Merlin!' she exclaimed.

Moonlight snorted and stepped forward to nuzzle the mysterious man, now seeming at ease. But Gwen still felt a bit confused. She had met Merlin once before, at a tournament at a nearby castle. Even though they had never met until that day, he had known her name, and all about her quest to save Avalon. He had given her advice that had helped her and Flora free Amelia the Silver Sister. But what was he doing here in the woods?

'What . . . what do you want?' she asked him.

'What do I want?' Merlin's shaggy eyebrows

rose slightly and a wry smile pulled at the corners of his mouth. 'I want peace and good fortune and for evil to be conquered. But wants are rarely met.'

Flora glanced uncertainly at Gwen, who flushed, feeling a little bit rude. She remembered from last time that Merlin often seemed to speak in riddles. 'Sorry – I meant, have you heard about the final Spell Sister? Is that why have you stopped us?'

The old man leant on his staff and regarded her with his eyes that reminded her of Nineve's – dark, deep and full of power. 'I have stopped you because I have a message for you, Guinevere. The road of your life is long, and you will face many twists and turns. You are only at the first bend of your journey now, but I am here to help you around it. It is vitally important that evil does not take Avalon today. You may need my help. In your darkest hour, illuminate the sky and call my name. I shall come.'

'I . . . I don't understand,' said Gwen in confusion.

'I know you do not understand right now – you must continue a little further before you will,' Merlin said gently. 'Now, be on your way. The Lady of the Lake is waiting. Give her my heartfelt greeting. But first . . .' He frowned. 'You are missing something, I see.'

'Missing something?' Gwen frowned.

'Your bow and arrows. You must have a way of protecting yourself if you are to face Morgana Le Fay.'

'Oh.' Gwen thought longingly about her bow and quiver of arrows back in her bedchamber at the castle. They were her most precious possessions. She carried them with her whenever she could, but she had left them in her chamber that afternoon, not wanting to anger her aunt by taking them to the rehearsal. She wished she could go back to the castle and get them, but she remembered the urgency in Nineve's eyes. 'We haven't got time to fetch them now, Merlin,' she said. 'We have to get to the Lake.'

'Then it is doubly fortunate you met me!' he said, his eyes shining.

Merlin nodded his head once and suddenly Gwen's bow and quiver of arrows were there in her hands. She gasped as fingers closed around the smooth elm-wood of the bow and soft leather quiver stuffed full of feather-tipped arrows. 'Oh my goodness! Thank you!' she said in awe as she slipped the bow over her shoulders and tied the quiver to the leather belt around her waist. Now she felt ready for any adventure!

'It is my pleasure,' Merlin replied. 'I hope you do not need them, but I fear you will before the day is over. Now, head for the Lake.' He reached over and touched Moonlight's nose. 'Carry them with all speed, my friend,' he whispered.

Before Gwen and Flora could say goodbye to Merlin, the stallion had plunged forward. Hanging on to Flora's waist, Gwen glanced back over her shoulder. The place where Merlin had been standing was now empty.

'He's gone! Wasn't it amazing how he conjured my bow and arrows?'

'Incredible. But what did all that stuff he said mean?' cried Flora over the thunder of Moonlight's hooves.

Gwen didn't know. But she had the feeling they would find out soon enough.

In your darkest hour, illuminate the sky and call my name. Remembering Merlin's words sent an icy shiver ran down her spine.

What was it that he knew they were facing? What was waiting for them in the hours ahead?

3

A Picture in the Lake

As Moonlight got closer to the Lake, rain started to fall. By the time they reached the Lake, hard drops were pelting into Gwen and Flora, who looked down at her dress in dismay. The stallion halted near the water and they quickly jumped off his back. Moonlight trotted off to take shelter in the trees as the girls ran to the Lake's edge. Dark clouds were hanging over the water and the rain was pouring down now.

As they stepped onto the black rocks surrounding the water, the Lake parted and Nineve rose up from the depths. 'Guinevere, Flora! You have come!'

'This rain is awful, Nineve!' said Flora shivering and pulling her cloak closely around her.

'It is Morgana's doing,' Nineve said. 'She is trying to prove that she still has much power. She can still control the weather using Chloe's stolen magic, so until Chloe is free you must take great care. Morgana will be more determined than ever to stop you from succeeding.'

Gwen lifted her chin, raindrops catching on her eyelashes. 'We don't care. Where is Chloe trapped, Nineve?'

Nineve waved one hand and a small cloud suddenly appeared on her palm. It floated down to the Lake's surface. Nineve whispered a soft word and the cloud turned a glowing purple before fading away. The place in the water where the little cloud had been hovering over stayed clear of raindrops and still.

Gwen and Flora leaned forwards eagerly as a picture formed in the water.

'Look closely! This is where I believe you will find Chloe the Storm Sister,' said Nineve.

Gwen frowned as she saw the inside of a stone chapel – a very familiar chapel with dusty stained glass windows and a thick oak door. 'That's the chapel in the woods near the castle where Cousin Bethany is getting married. We've just come from there!'

Nineve looked at both of the girls with

surprise.

'Is Chloe really trapped in there?' said Flora, her eyes wide.

The Lady of the Lake nodded. 'That is what my magic tells me.'

'But we were in the chapel for ages,' said Flora. 'I didn't see her.'

'We weren't really looking though,' said Gwen slowly. 'Just think about how well Morgana has hidden the other sisters. Chloe could have been trapped absolutely anywhere in the chapel – in one of the walls, the stones in the floor even in the wooden doors.'

'Guinevere is right,' said Nineve. 'Morgana always disguises the sisters when she imprisons them. I am sure Chloe is in this chapel somewhere.'

'Then we'll go back and find her!' said Flora.

'Yes!' agreed Gwen. 'We'll go there right

now. At least it's not far away.'

'Please be aware of the danger,' warned Nineve, her eyes anxious. 'There is no knowing what Morgana has planned. She will most certainly have placed protective spells on Chloe.'

Gwen thought of all the ways Morgana had tried to stop them in the past – hornets, wolves, tidal waves . . . She knew Morgana would do absolutely everything she could to stop them from freeing the final Spell Sister. *Well, she's not going to,* Gwen thought determinedly. *We're going to save Avalon and Morgana isn't going to stop us!*

'We'll be careful and we'll be back with Chloe as soon as we can,' she told Nineve.

'Bye, Nineve!' Flora said.

She and Gwen raced back through the rain towards where Moonlight was sheltering in the trees. They climbed on to his back and turned to Nineve who was waving a goodbye from the Lake. They both waved to her and then Gwen wrapped her arms around Flora's waist.

'Back to the chapel, Moonlight!' she cried.

With a wild whinny, the stallion galloped off through the rain-soaked trees.

✦ ✦ ✦

With everyone now returned to the castle, the chapel and the clearing surrounding it was eerily quiet when they got there. Gwen and Flora dismounted and left Moonlight in the trees, just in case anyone decided to come back. They both knew they would never be able to explain how they came to have such a magnificent stallion or how they could ride him without a saddle or bridle.

Moonlight whinnied as they walked away from him. Gwen had the strangest feeling he was wishing them good luck.

It wasn't raining, but clouds seemed to be pressing down on the chapel and the surrounding woods. Now all the people had gone, Gwen noticed a heavy, still feeling in the air – she knew it meant that dangerous magic had been worked there. Gwen tried not to let it weaken her resolve. They had to find Chloe.

'This is it,' she told Flora determinedly. 'The last Spell Sister. We're going to free her and save Avalon.'

Flora nodded determinedly and twisted the metal handle on the wooden door to the chapel.

Gwen checked the door thoroughly as it swung open, in case Chloe was trapped inside it, but there was no hint of a girl's face or body in the grain of the wood.

Flora started examining the pews, while Gwen checked the stone floor. Everything looked completely ordinary.

'Where can she be?' Gwen said, walking up and down the chapel.

'I don't know,' said Flora, kneeling down and checking under a pew.

Gwen inspected the stone pillars on either side of the aisle, they were smooth, no sign of a hidden Spell Sister at all. She frowned. So Chloe wasn't trapped in the door, the floor, the pillars, or the pews. Maybe she was in the roof,

or maybe . . . Gwen turned and looked at the stained glass windows.

The light filtered through the different coloured glass. Most of the windows were dusty, showing pictures of pilgrims and religious stories. But Gwen looked towards the window she had noticed earlier as being newer and cleaner than the others. Gwen had been so busy thinking about Nineve that she hadn't looked properly at the picture in the glass earlier on, but now, she went over and studied it.

Instead of a religious scene, the window had a picture of a beautiful girl with long silver hair. She was clearly backing away from something – or someone – her face terrified, her arms reaching up to shield her face.

'Flora! Over here!' she gasped, pointing upwards, 'I think it's Chloe!'

Flora ran over to where Gwen was standing and clutched her arm. 'Oh Gwen, free her quickly!'

Gwen pulled the pendant out from round her neck. She needed to press it to the image and say the special spell Nineve had taught her to release a trapped Spell Sister. But she couldn't reach the stained glass window. 'I need something to stand on!'

Flora spotted some old wooden chairs at the back of the chapel and dragged one over. Gwen stood on it. It wobbled slightly on the uneven floor, but she took no notice. Her eyes were fixed on the girl. Were they right? Had they really found Chloe the Storm Sister?

Morgana's Dangerous Magic

Clutching the pendant, Gwen leant closer. Heart pounding, she touched the pendant to the stained glass and called out:

'Spell Sister of Avalon I now release
Return to the island and help bring peace!'

A bright flash immediately lit up the gloomy chapel. Silvery light swirled out of nowhere and swept across the surface of the stained glass. As it cleared, all the colourful panes shone like glittering jewels. The outline of the girl grew clearer and clearer until suddenly she floated right out of the glass!

'It's Chloe!' cried Flora.

Gwen half expected the doors of the chapel to slam shut or furniture to start magically hurling itself at them as the sister floated down and landed beside her. But nothing dangerous happened at all. Could Nineve have been wrong? Perhaps Morgana had not placed any spells of protection around the sister this time. Gwen certainly hoped so, but she knew they had to stay alert, just in case.

The tall, slim girl looked at Gwen and Flora

nervously. Her hair was long and silver, her eyes a deep turquoise in colour. She had a circlet of blue stones on her head and was wearing a dress that glimmered in shades of silver, white and grey. 'Wh-Who are you?' she asked.

'It's OK, Chloe, we're friends. We've been sent by Nineve to rescue you,' said Gwen, quickly slipping the necklace back over her head. 'I'm Guinevere, and this is Flora.'

'Nineve saw where you were using her magic,' Flora put in. 'She sent us to free you so you can get back to Avalon.'

'There isn't much time,' said Gwen quickly. 'Morgana is going to try and cross the Lake and get to the island this evening. You need to be back on Avalon with all your sisters if she is to be stopped.'

Chloe looked anxious. 'My sisters?' she

asked. 'Are they all right?'

'Yes. We have helped them all escape from Morgana and they're waiting for you back on the island.'

'I must go there at once!' said Chloe, her face lighting up. 'Oh, thank you for rescuing me! Thank you so much!'

'It's been no problem,' smiled Gwen. And she realised how true the words were. This was the easiest rescue of all the Spell Sisters.

Chloe's eyes fell on Gwen's necklace. 'I see each of my sisters has given you a gift,' she said with a smile. 'It seems only right I should give you one of my own before I return to my home.'

She clasped her hands lightly together. There was faint pattering sound like rain falling and then she opened her hands to reveal a beautiful raindrop-shaped diamond. It glittered brightly in the sunlight. 'Here,' she said.

'Thank you!' Gwen breathed. Chloe whispered a word and the diamond drop floated upwards and attached itself to her necklace with a silver flash. Gwen touched the chain. Now she had the pendant and eight gems – one from each Spell Sister.

'I must go now,' said Chloe.

Gwen nodded. 'We'll follow you on our stallion Moonlight. We'll see you back at the La—'

'I think not!' a harsh voice snapped, interrupting them.

They all swung round. Flora squeaked in fear. A tall dark haired woman was standing in the chapel doorway. Her hooded cloak reached the ground and she had a staff of dark wood in her hand.

Chloe turned pale. 'Morgana!' she whispered.

Morgana Le Fay glared at her. 'Yes,' she hissed. 'You will not escape, Chloe. None of you will.'

Gwen's mouth went dry. What was the sorceress planning on doing? She forced down her fear. 'Stay away from us!' she shouted, stepping forwards bravely.

Morgana's lip curled. 'Willingly. I have no need to waste my time harming you – tempting though the idea is. Instead I shall simply trap you here. Then once the eclipse begins, the island of Avalon will become mine and the seven Spell Sisters who are there now will be expelled from it forever.'

'Trap us?' Flora quavered.

Morgana tossed back her hair and laughed.

'Yes.' Her voice rose. 'My magic will mean no one inside this chapel shall leave this place until after the lunar eclipse. I will use all my power to command it!' She lifted her staff high over her head. There was a violent crash of thunder, and then as quickly as she had appeared, Morgana vanished.

At the same moment, the oak door slammed shut and iron bars sprang out of the walls, covering the windows.

'Oh, no!' Chloe cried in dismay.

As the thunder faded, Gwen ran forwards and grabbed the metal ring on the door, tugging and twisting desperately – but it wouldn't move. She looked around the chapel, hoping to find another exit, but there was no other way out. All of the windows were barred and blocked. They were stuck inside.

'What are we going to do?' Flora asked urgently.

'This is terrible I've got to get back to Avalon before Morgana ruins everything!' said Chloe, running and trying the door too.

Gwen's thoughts raced. She suddenly remembered something. 'It's all right. You can magic yourself there! You don't need us. Go to the Lake and speak to Nineve. She'll help you get to the island and then you can fight off Morgana with your sisters.'

Chloe hesitated. 'But

what about you two?'

'We'll be safe here,' said Gwen. 'Morgana won't worry about us. She'll be too busy thinking about getting to the island. Her spell on the door can't last forever.'

'You must go, Chloe,' begged Flora. 'Gwen's right. We'll be fine. Avalon has to be saved – your sisters need you.'

Chloe nodded, her eyebrows still knitted with worry. 'Very well. I believe you will be safe here. I shall use my magic to return to Avalon. Thank you for freeing me!'

She ran to them and kissed them both on the cheek then she lifted her hands and clapped them together. 'To the Lake!' she cried.

Nothing happened.

Gwen frowned. All of the other sisters had been able to use their magic to return to the Lake when they had been freed.

'To the Lake!' Chloe repeated desperately. But there was no flash of light, no magic. Chloe slowly lowered her hands. 'My magic,' she whispered, looking stricken. 'It's not working.'

'It . . . it must!' stammered Flora.

But no matter how hard Chloe tried she couldn't magic herself away to the Lake.

Gwen felt dread prickle across her skin as she suddenly realised what was going on. 'Of course. Morgana would know you would use your magic to escape. Her spell must be a very powerful one, not just blocking the doors and windows, but stopping your magic too. We're all trapped here!'

They stared at each other in horror.

'My sisters . . . Avalon . . .' whispered Chloe. 'They're doomed.'

'No,' said Gwen, refusing to be beaten. 'They're not. We'll find a way out. We have to!'

5

The Darkest Hour

wen paced around the chapel. If only she could think of a way to at least allow Chloe to escape. They had to get her back to Avalon as soon as possible. Flora was sitting down next to the Spell Sister who had tears falling quietly down her cheeks. Flora had her arm around her and was looking very upset herself. They were so close to stopping Morgana – Gwen knew they couldn't give up now.

But what can we do? Gwen thought for the hundredth time as she paced up and down the chapel's aisle. Looking up to the stained glass windows, she could tell that the light was fading outside. The sun was setting. Time was running out. *It'll be dark soon,* she thought worriedly.

Dark . . .

The word rang a bell in her head. She sifted through her memories trying to work out why it seemed important. What was it about the word dark?

Suddenly words popped into her head.

In your darkest hour . . .

Merlin! Of course! He had told her: *In your darkest hour, illuminate the sky and call my name. I shall come.*

Gwen felt a leap of hope. It sounded like

Merlin had meant for them to shine a light into the sky as a way of sending him a message. Her hope faded. But how could they do that when they were trapped inside the chapel?

'Oh!' she exclaimed in frustration.

'What?' Flora asked.

Gwen sighed and told her what she had been thinking. 'But there's no way of getting a message to Merlin. How on earth are we going to light up the sky from in here?'

'I can!' said Chloe jumping to her feet. 'Now I am free, my weather powers have come back to me. I could make a fork of lightning flash across the sky, and we could call Merlin that way!'

'But how would he know it was us calling him?' said Flora, confused.

'All we need to do is call his name,' said Chloe, her eyes shining. 'He is very special. He will hear our call, and know we need him.'

'But will he be able to help?' said Gwen.

'Yes, I'm sure of it! Merlin has very special powers, just like Nineve. He must have had a feeling you would have need of him tonight, or he wouldn't have told you to call on him.'

Gwen grabbed her hand. 'Then let's send him a message!'

Chloe strode to the nearest window and lifted her hands.

'In the sky forge a fork of light
To carry a message across the night!'

Through the window the girls saw a bright flash of lightning tear down across the sky. 'Merlin!' Gwen yelled. 'Merlin we need your help. Please come!'

Chloe and Flora joined in, their voices ringing through the stone chapel. 'MERLIN!'

The lightning faded.

There was silence.

'Now what?' Gwen said. They looked at one another, waiting.

Then, all of a sudden, there were two loud bangs of a staff on the oak door. The girls almost jumped out of their skin. What if it was Morgana, returning to stop them from summoning the mysterious man?

But to Gwen's relief she heard Merlin's voice. 'You called me. I have come.'

Gwen ran to the door. 'Merlin! Morgana has put a spell on the chapel. We're trapped in here and Chloe can't get back to Avalon.

Can you get her out?'

'Yes, but it will take great power,' came Merlin's reply. 'I sense that the spell on this chapel is very strong. Chloe, Storm Sister of Avalon, will you help me to break the spell that holds you here against your will?'

'Of course! I'll do anything,' Chloe cried.

'Then you must use your magic to create a storm in the sky, and I shall harness its power. Together we can destroy Morgana's spell.'

Gwen took one of Flora's hands as Chloe started chanting her own spell. For now, the girls could only watch. 'Please let this work,' Flora whispered.

Gwen bit her lip. *Please, please,* she prayed.

Chloe raised her hands aloft and called out in a clear voice:

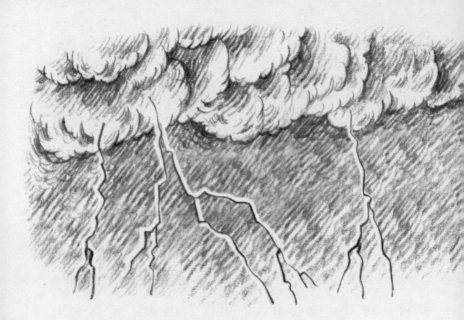

'Thunder loud and lightning bright
Come together on this dark night.'

Through the chinks in the glass, Gwen could see that dark clouds were meeting over the chapel. Then lightning began to flash, and there was the roll and crash of thunder. The chapel seemed to shake with every thunderclap. Gwen felt the power rolling over the stone building.

Outside, she heard Merlin's voice rising above the storm.

'From the storm above, power I take,
I use it now, a spell to break!'

There was an enormous flash of light. For a second, every inch of the chapel seemed to shine and then the light disappeared and the door flew open. Merlin stood on the threshold. Sparks of silver glowed in his long grey hair, and his staff was still held aloft.

'You did it, Merlin!' Gwen gasped. 'You broke the spell!'

'We did it together,' said Merlin, his eyes meeting Chloe's. 'Thank you, Spell Sister of Avalon.'

Chloe smiled back.

'Be quick,' Merlin said quickly. 'You must leave this place now. As soon as Morgana realises her spell has been broken she will return, and you do not want to be here when she does.' He beckoned to them and they ran out of the chapel into the rain.

'I shall return to my sisters,' said Chloe quickly.

Outside the full moon was rising in the sky.

'Go with all speed,' Merlin said. 'The time of the eclipse approaches. When the moon is fully shadowed, Nineve's spell of protection on the Lake will fade. You must be ready to fight Morgana then.'

Chloe nodded. 'We will do all we can!' She hugged Gwen and Flora. 'Goodbye, girls. See you soon.'

'Goodbye!' they gasped.

'To the Lake!' she cried as she finally disappeared in a swirl of silver light.

Gwen felt a rush of relief. Chloe's magic had finally worked!

Merlin stepped forwards. 'The eighth Spell Sister has returned, but the danger is not over yet. Morgana must not take Avalon. Will you do all in your power to help our friends tonight?'

Gwen and Flora nodded hard.

'Then go to the Lake as quickly as you can. Your help will be needed.'

'But how can we help? We're not able to perform magic or cast spells,' said Flora.

'Do not underestimate yourselves,' Merlin said softly.

He whistled and Moonlight came trotting out of the trees.

Merlin helped Flora up on to the stallion's back. Gwen needed no help. She vaulted up behind Flora, her heart beating wildly in her chest. The danger to Avalon wasn't over yet, and whatever she could do to help, she would do it.

'Remember the fate of the kingdom rests in your hands tonight.' Merlin's dark eyes found Gwen's. 'You may not be aware of it now, but you carry great power and you know all you need to.'

Gwen had no idea what he meant. 'Are you coming with us, Merlin?' she asked hopefully.

'No,' he said sadly. 'I cannot. I have played my part in this story for now. The rest is up to you, Nineve and the Spell Sisters. May the magic of Avalon keep you safe and help you triumph over evil tonight.'

And with that, he was gone. The place he had been standing was empty and now the only sign that Merlin had been there at all were a few leaves that stirred on the ground.

'Merlin!' Flora gasped. 'Come back!'

'He won't,' said Gwen, knowing it with a cold certainty. 'It's up to us now, Flora. We have to go and help the Spell Sisters.' Gwen touched her heels to Moonlight's sides. 'To the Lake, Moonlight, as fast as you can take us!'

The stallion leapt forwards and sped swiftly through the trees.

A Very Special Spell

Moonlight galloped faster than ever to the Lake. He burst through the trees and into the clearing near the water. As he skidded to a halt, his hooves threw up a spray of fallen leaves. The girls jumped off his back and Gwen started running towards the Lake, but as she did so Moonlight gave a high-pitched whinny of fear.

'Gwen!' Flora shrieked from beside him. 'Look.'

Gwen stopped, her eyes taking in the scene. Morgana Le Fay was standing on the rocks near the water, her pale face lit by the moonlight.

Standing next to her was Chloe. Her eyes were flicking desperately from side to side, but she didn't move or speak. Gwen suddenly realised a spell must be holding the Spell Sister in place – binding her invisibly. There was no sign of Nineve. Where was she?

A shiver of fear ran through Gwen as Morgana glared icily toward her and Flora.

'So, you have decided to join us. You girls who have caused me so many problems. Well, now you can see that all your efforts have been for nothing! You thought you had freed Chloe, but I was waiting here in case you found a way to break my spell and now I have caught her again. There are still only seven Spell Sisters on Avalon, and that will not be enough to stop me. A short while from now, when the moon is covered completely by shadow, I shall cross the Lake and take control of the island at long last!'

Gwen saw the triumph in Morgana's eyes, and anger swept away her fear. 'No you won't! We'll stop you!' she said, marching forward.

'Gwen!' gasped Flora, running forwards and grabbing her arm. '*Sssh!*'

Morgana's arched eyebrows rose. 'You should listen to your little friend and hold your tongue,' she snapped at Gwen. 'How exactly do you plan to stop me? You have no powers, no magic of your own. You're just a child. You cannot rely on the Spell Sisters' powers to help you now.'

Gwen bit her lip. She was right. What could she do to stop a powerful sorceress like Morgana?

Morgana laughed scornfully. 'You are no threat to me! Now watch me take the island you have tried so hard to save. Nineve's magic is already weaker and I can at last cast my spells and claim Avalon.'

She turned to the island and slowly raised her hands.

As Morgana turned away from them, Flora gave a strangled squeak and pointed at Gwen's chest. Gwen followed her gaze. The pendant was glowing!

A mist swirled across the surface. Gwen hurried away from where Morgana was facing the Lake preparing to cast her spell and peered into the pendant, with Flora quickly rushing to her side.

'Nineve,' Gwen whispered desperately as she saw the Lady of the Lake's face shimmer into view. She glanced up to check Morgana's back was still turned. 'Are you all right? Where are you?'

'I am in the Lake,' Nineve said, her voice quick and desperate. 'I am trying to keep up the protection spell, so I cannot come to you now. I must keep the spell strong for as long as I possibly can. Do everything you can to stop Morgana before the shadow covers the moon and my spell fades!'

Flora tugged Gwen's arm. 'Look!' she said in alarm. 'What's Morgana doing now?'

The sorceress was pointing her staff at the mist hiding Avalon. Standing beside her, still bound by Morgana's evil magic, Chloe struggled, but couldn't break free.

'I must go!' said Nineve hastily. 'I can feel Morgana is about to work more magic. Do all you can to help, Guinevere!'

Her image faded.

Beside the Lake, the girls heard Morgana begin to call out a spell.

Eight sisters are needed, but only seven now stand fast
Evil can defeat them and darkness win at last.
It is time to leave the island, sisters hear my command
Walk from the shores of Avalon, leave your precious land.

Gwen caught her breath. The mist around Avalon started to swirl faster and faster before it suddenly disappeared. The island was revealed, its green slopes crisscrossed with small streams, a sandy beach and a path leading to a stone house with brightly lit windows.

'What's Morgana doing?' Flora whispered anxiously.

Gwen didn't know. But as they watched, an invisible hand seemed to open the front door of the house.

There was a moment's pause, and then the seven Spell Sisters came filing out of the house. Their eyes were blank, their arms hanging by their sides. They moved silently as if in a trance. Gwen felt sick as she realised that Morgana was controlling the sisters against their will – making them leave the island by using her evil powers. If they were forced from Avalon, the sorceress would be able to take the island with no resistance when Nineve's spell was broken.

Gwen's thoughts tumbled through her mind desperately as she watched the Spell Sisters walk out of the house and down to the Lake in single file. There was Sophia the Flame Sister, who they had rescued first. Following her was Isabella the Butterfly Sister and Amelia the Silver Sister. Then came Lily the Forest Sister, Grace the Sea Sister, Evie the Swan Sister and finally Olivia the Otter Sister, who they had rescued only a few days ago.

As Sophia stepped on to the surface of the Lake and began to walk across it as if it was dry land, Gwen took a deep breath and pushed her shoulders back. She and Flora had fought too hard to let Morgana win now. Gwen knew she had to stop what was happening. She might not be able to do magic, but she did have her bow and arrows, maybe she could use her archery skills to stop Morgana.

Pulling her bow over her head, she grabbed a feather-tipped arrow from the quiver and notched it onto the bowstring. Raising the bow, she pulled the string back, anchoring it for a moment against her cheek. Then she took aim at the sorceress and let the arrow fly.

The arrow shot towards Morgana.

For a moment, Gwen thought it was going to hit her, but at the last second Morgana seemed to sense it and shouted a command, raising her hand. It was as though Morgana had conjured an unseen shield – the arrow rebounded away from her and fell harmlessly to the ground. Gwen frowned, but she didn't give up. She shot another arrow and then a third. One ripped a hole in the hood of Morgana's cloak, another just missed her arm as the sorceress tried to deflect the rapidly fired arrows.

'Enough of this!' Morgana snapped angrily.

Swinging round, she pointed a finger at Gwen and muttered an evil-sounding spell.

Invisible ropes suddenly seemed to tighten around Gwen's arms, squeezing hard. Her muscles felt as if they had turned to lead. Her hands fell to her sides. The bow felt much too heavy to lift.

Morgana laughed mockingly. 'Stupid girl. Did you really think you could stop me with your silly arrows?'

'What's the matter, Gwen?' shouted Flora anxiously.

'My arms! Morgana's cast a spell on me!' Gwen tried to force her arms upwards, but it was so hard – her muscles trembled with the effort.

Morgana pointed upwards. Following her gaze, Gwen saw that a shadow was starting to creep across the pale disc of the moon. 'The eclipse has started!' the sorceress crowed.

The sisters had almost reached Morgana at the Lake's edge. Gwen watched helplessly as the first of them, Sophia, stepped off the water on to the rocks.

Despair filled her. There really was nothing she could do. She had tried her hardest, but she was all out of ideas. Merlin had been wrong. There was no way she could help to stop what was about to happen.

'Gwen!' cried Flora, watching as the second Spell Sister stepped on to the rocks. 'We've got to do something!'

'There's nothing we can do,' Gwen said miserably. 'I don't carry great power at all. What Merlin said wasn't true!'

'Carry . . . ?' Flora's eyes widened to the size of dinner plates. *'Carry it!'* she said. 'Of course! Oh, Gwen that's it! Merlin didn't mean that you have great power like him and Nineve, or magic like each of the sisters. He meant that you *carry* the sisters' powers!'

Gwen looked at her in confusion. 'What? I don't understand.'

'Your necklace! It has eight gemstones, one from each of the Spell Sisters. They each gave a gem to you, saying that you might have need of it one day. I bet the *gems* are magic!'

Gwen looked down at the necklace and the gems that surrounded the blue pendant.

But even if Flora was right, even if the gems

had the Spell Sisters' magic in them, what could she do with it? She didn't know how to make them work.

You know all you need. Merlin's voice echoed in Gwen's head.

It's not true, she thought. I only know one spell – the spell of release . . .

Her heart skipped a beat as something suddenly occurred to her. Maybe that was what Merlin meant? The spell she had been taught had freed each of the Spell Sisters from Morgana's clutches when she had trapped them before. Maybe the same spell would also release whatever magic was held in the gemstones? Gwen didn't know if it would, but she suddenly knew she had to try. She glanced up to the sky, and the moon was now just a sliver of light, almost totally covered in shadow. The eclipse would begin any moment.

Gwen reached for the necklace. Every muscle in her arms hurt. *Give up,* a dangerous part of her mind whispered, but she fought against it. Gritting her teeth and ignoring the pain, she finally managed to grasp the pendant and angle it towards the sky. The final ray of moonlight caught it just before the moon disappeared completely from view.

'*Sisters of Avalon, I now release!*' Gwen whispered intently. '*Return to the island and help bring peace!*'

Her heart pounded as all eight gemstones began to glow and sparkle. Suddenly, a blazing beam shot out of the centre of each of gem, swirling upwards in a glittering, multi-coloured cloud of magic lighting up the sky. The magic spun around above Gwen's head and she felt as

if she was glowing and crackling with energy. Her arms felt free again and all the magic of the Spell Sisters flowed through her necklace. White orchids bloomed at her feet, rainbow-coloured butterflies flew around her head, tiny songbirds perched on her shoulders, silver dust fell around her and flames sparked from her hands.

Morgana swung round. 'NO!' she shrieked. But it was too late. The necklace's magic shot straight towards her.

7
Saving Avalon

The glittering cloud of magic from Gwen's necklace surrounded Morgana and the eight Spell Sisters. As it touched each of the sisters, Morgana's spell lifted, and they blinked and came out of their trance. They all looked furious.

'Morgana! You shall not take Avalon!' cried Sophia. She lifted her hands. 'Fire help me!'

she shouted.

'Hornets come to my aid!' cried Isabella beside her, her eyes flashing.

'Birds of the night be with me!' cried Evie.

'Lightning strike from the sky!' shouted Chloe.

A ball of flames shot from Sophia's fingers straight towards the sorceress and a fork of lightning tore down through the sky, but Morgana deflected both with a silvery magical shield. The next second, a cloud of angry hornets were swarming towards her and birds were swooping down from the night sky, talons out, curved beaks open.

Morgana fired green flames at the birds and insects,

which swerved away. But the Spell Sisters were not defeated yet.

'Metal rise from the ground!' cried Amelia.

'Wave sweep up from the Lake!' shouted Grace.

Gwen's fallen arrows abruptly rose from the floor, their metal tips suddenly glowing. They shot through the air towards Morgana, making her duck and dodge. Meanwhile the waters of the Lake rose up in a tidal wave and headed straight for the rocks where Morgana was standing. Seeing the wall of water bearing down on her, she turned and started to flee. The wave crashed

down on the rocks, turning to harmless water droplets around Grace's feet.

'Creatures of the woods attack!' shouted Olivia.

'Bindweed grow and twist!' shouted Lily.

There was a yowling and a barking as foxes and wild cats came running out of the woods, teeth bared and claws out as they blocked Morgana's escape. At the same time, long strands of tough green bindweed rushed across the ground and rose up to curl around Morgana's ankles and legs, stopping her in her tracks.

Morgana spat a curse at the bindweed. It blackened and fell away, but almost immediately new tendrils snaked upwards and twisted around her.

The wild animals surrounded her. The noise was deafening. Gwen and Flora reached one another amid the chaos and grasped hands.

In front of them, Morgana finally gave a despairing cry and clapped her palms together. A crash of thunder echoed out around them, and the evil sorceress disappeared, leaving just a clump of blackened bindweed on the floor. The woodland animals leaped on the spot where she had been standing, but she had well and truly vanished.

For a moment there was silence.

'She's . . . she's gone,' stammered Gwen.

'And she failed! She didn't manage to take Avalon!' said Flora in delight.

'Is it really over?' whispered Gwen, hardly daring to believe it.

As she spoke, the shadows passed over the moon and it appeared in the sky again as a thin crescent floating in the darkness.

'Yes, it would seem so,' Sophia said, a smile breaking out in her face as she looked over at Gwen and Flora. 'It is over!'

All the Spell Sisters started to talk and laugh and hug each other.

'You saved the day!' said Chloe, hurrying to the girls and embracing them. 'You released the magic in the stones and freed us. Morgana has gone. Thank you so much!'

'I didn't do anything, it was Gwen,' said Flora. 'She was the one who chanted the spell.'

'But it was you who realised what Merlin meant, Flora,' Gwen replied. 'Without you, I never would have thought of using the necklace.'

'Everyone played their part,' said Chloe

with a smile.

'It was amazing,' said Flora. 'There was so much magic!'

Olivia ran to where the foxes and wild cats were milling round. She crouched down and stroked their soft coats as they pushed their heads against her legs. 'Thank you, my friends,' she said softly. 'Go now, in peace.' They nuzzled her and trotted back to their homes in the woods.

The birds circled around Isabella on their large wings. 'Fly free!' she called to them and they flew away, swooping silently through the night and back into the shadows.

The clouds were clearing from the moon now. Pale light shone down, and a silver ripple ran over the entire surface of the Lake as the waters parted.

'Nineve!' cried Grace in delight as the

Lady of the Lake rose up from the water. She was smiling, her dark eyes alight, her long chestnut hair falling over her shoulders and down to her feet. 'My friends!' she cried, holding her arms wide. 'Avalon has been saved! Morgana shall not use it's magic to bring misery to the kingdom. Now the island can truly be a place of happiness once again. Come, let us go and celebrate there!'

A fine white mist rose from the Lake's surface. It swirled around everyone's feet, spiralling up from their toes, around their legs. Gwen and Flora felt themselves being lifted into the air. The mist carried them gently on to the Lake and set them down on its surface. But they didn't sink – they could walk across the water! In the centre of the Lake, they saw the island of Avalon waiting for them, the lights in the house window glowing cheerfully, welcoming the Spell Sisters home.

The sisters ran lightly across the water onto Avalon's welcoming shores. Gwen and Flora held hands with the Lady of the Lake and the three of them began to follow on to the house as well.

'Nineve!' Gwen exclaimed. 'You're out of the Lake. I thought you couldn't leave the water?'

'I couldn't because I had to make sure the spell of protection remained strong, but now all the Spell Sisters have returned, I am able to once more step on to the island,' said Nineve.

Gwen squeezed her hand happily and they all smiled at one another. As they stepped on to the sandy beach, and looked at the green island with its glittering streams and fruit-laden apple trees, the final shadows slipped from the moon

and the whole island seemed to glitter with silver light.

Gwen remembered what the island had looked like when she and Flora had first seen it, the day she had pulled the pendant out of the rock. Back then it had been barren and bare, the apple trees leafless, the house deserted, the streams dried up. But as each of the Spell Sisters had returned, the island had begun to heal itself, and now apples hung from the branches of the trees, flowers covered the grass and the streams bubbled with clear water. It was positively shining with magic.

We really did it, Gwen thought in awe. *Flora and I rescued all of the sisters and saved Avalon from Morgana.* She caught Flora's gaze and knew she was thinking the same thing. Smiling at each other, they followed the sisters up the path to the brightly-lit house.

Once inside, Sophia relit a roaring fire in the grate while Evie conjured a host of songbirds which perched on the curtain rails and sang sweetly. Lily made roses, freesia and lilies bloom on the mantelpiece, filling the air with a delicate fragrance. The other sisters laid out a feast on the large wooden kitchen table. There were silver bowls of ripe fruit, jugs of punch and gold plates of delicious honey biscuits and iced cakes. Everyone laughed and chatted as they handed round the food and drink.

Sophia turned to Gwen and Flora and smiled. Her hair, red as flames, framed her pale face. 'We cannot thank you enough, girls. When you first freed me and I came back here to live on my own, I despaired and thought that there was no hope that my sisters would ever be free. I believed Morgana would take the island. But you never gave up. You rescued every single one of us.'

The other Spell Sisters nodded in agreement.

'It's true. We owe our lives to you,' said Olivia softly. 'We would still have been trapped if you hadn't freed us.'

'And Avalon would have become Morgana's,' added Chloe with a shiver.

'I'm just glad we were able to help,' said Gwen, grinning round at them all.

Flora nodded. 'Me too. When Gwen first pulled the pendant out of the rock I thought I didn't want to have adventures! I couldn't have been more wrong.'

Gwen's hand went to the silver chain around her neck. 'I suppose I should give the pendant back to you now, Nineve,' she said. She felt a sad tug at her heart as she spoke. She loved the necklace with the big blue pendant, but it belonged to Nineve. She started to pull it over her head but Nineve stopped her.

'No, Guinevere. Please keep it as a thank you gift. Also, I may need to contact you again one day, and so it is right that it stays with you.

And Flora, you should also have something too, to show our gratitude. Here.' She clasped her hands for a moment, whispered a word and then opened them to reveal a delicate bracelet with silver links and small blue gems that matched Flora's eyes. Nineve blew on it. It floated magically into the air. There was a silver flash and Flora blinked as the bracelet clasped itself around her wrist.

'It's beautiful!' Flora breathed. 'Thank you!'

'Thank you,' said Nineve. 'To you both, for all you have done, for the determination, cleverness and, most of all, the courage you have shown.'

The sisters murmured in agreement. Then Sophia smiled. 'Now, this is supposed to be a party. We should have some music and dancing!'

Amelia conjured a silver flute and started to play a lively tune. The other sisters pushed the chairs back, and everyone started to dance around the kitchen. As the shadow swept away from the moon above, music and laughter rang out of the house. Avalon was a place of happiness once again.

8

Time to Celebrate!

At long last it was time for the girls to return to the castle. 'I hope everyone at home hasn't been too worried about us,' said Flora as she and Gwen left the house on Avalon and walked back down the path towards the Lake. 'We're going to get into so much trouble. We've not been home since the rehearsal and it must be past midnight now.'

'Do not worry, I think Merlin may have helped you with a spell,' said Nineve with a knowing smile. She had accompanied them back down to the water's edge. 'I wouldn't be surprised if you get back and find you hadn't been missed at all. If people thought about you, their thoughts would have instantly slipped on to something else before they could start to worry.'

Gwen and Flora sighed in relief. It was good to know they would be able to get back to the castle with their absence having gone unnoticed.

They stepped on to the surface of the Lake. 'Goodbye!' all the Spell Sisters called. 'And thank you again!'

'Goodbye!' Flora and Gwen waved back and then they headed out across the Lake with Nineve. As they reached the other side, they waved once more, and then Nineve whispered a word and the island of Avalon was once again hidden from curious eyes by a thick purple mist.

'I'm so glad we could help,' said Flora as she stepped on to the rocks.

'Thank you.' Nineve embraced her and then Gwen, squeezing them both tightly. 'Now, take care of yourselves.'

A thought struck Gwen. 'Will we see you again, Nineve? This isn't goodbye forever, is it?'

Nineve smiled. 'No. Our paths will certainly cross again in the future. Keep the pendant safe, Guinevere. If I ever have need of help, I shall use it to call on you.'

'I'll keep it very safe,' promised Gwen.

Nineve kissed her cheek. 'Do not worry. Your adventures are not over, Guinevere,' she whispered into her ear. 'I can promise you that.'

Gwen and Flora stepped onto the rocky

shore beside the Lake. Nineve turned to wave at them once more before sinking down slowly into the shimmering blue depths. The water closed over her head.

For a long moment, the two girls stood in silence.

'It's strange. I'm happy but also sad,' said Flora. 'I'm pleased the Spell Sisters and Avalon are safe, but I really will miss having adventures!'

Gwen grinned. 'Flora! I never thought I would hear you say that.'

Flora giggled. 'I know, but actually I think life's going to be rather dull without any magical sisters to save.'

Gwen's eyes twinkled as she thought back over some of their adventures. 'Yes, I can see you're really going to miss ferocious wolves trying to eat us, hornets trying to sting us to death, wild horses trying to trample us, magical waves trying to drown us—'

'All right, all right.' Flora pulled a face. 'Maybe I won't miss some parts of the adventures!'

A whinny rang out from the trees. They swung round. Moonlight stepped out from the shadows and pawed the ground. It looked like he was waiting to take them back to the castle.

'I *will* miss Moonlight though,' Flora said softly.

'Me too,' sighed Gwen.

They went over and petted the stallion for several minutes before climbing on to his warm back.

'We don't need to gallop this time,' said Gwen, thinking about what Nineve had said about Merlin's spell on the castle. She hated the thought of saying goodbye to Moonlight, and even though she was now starting to feel very tired she wanted the journey home to take as long as possible. Moonlight walked and trotted through the trees until he came to a stop at the edge of the woods. The castle loomed on the hill in front of them, its turrets silhouetted in the moonlight.

Gwen dismounted and then helped Flora down too. 'It's time to say goodbye, Moonlight,' she said sadly.

Moonlight nuzzled her shoulder and then her hair. Gwen swallowed and put her arms round his neck, burying her face in his silky mane. She didn't want to let him go.

Flora stroked his soft nose. 'Couldn't we take him back to the castle?' she suggested longingly. 'We could say we found him in the woods.'

Gwen felt a surge of hope. Maybe they could? *Moonlight could live in the castle stables and they could groom him and ride him . . . and . . . and . . .* Her thoughts came to a halt. The reality hit her – girls weren't allowed to ride stallions like Moonlight. If they took him to the stables, he would undoubtedly become her uncle's horse. Moonlight would have to wear a saddle and bridle and learn to obey his rider's every command.

She looked at the beautiful stallion – at the wildness and intelligence in his eyes – and knew that no matter how much she wanted it, she couldn't take him to the stables. Moonlight was meant to be free.

'We can't,' she said softly to Flora. 'You know he'd hate life in the castle stables.' She stroked the stallion's forehead. 'You belong here in the woods, don't you, boy?' He rubbed his ears against her. Gwen felt a lump of tears in her throat but she forced herself to be strong. She stepped back.

'Go now, Moonlight,' she said softly. 'Stay wild in the woods.' She touched the pendant around her neck. 'We'll come and visit you here and we'll call on you if we ever need you to take us to the Lake.'

Moonlight stared back at her, his dark eyes as deep as forest pools and then he nodded. With a soft whicker of goodbye, he turned and trotted into the trees.

Flora swallowed, tears shining in her eyes.

'Come on,' said Gwen, squeezing her hand. 'It's time for us to go home too.'

✦ ✦ ✦

They hurried back up the hill to the castle. To their surprise, people weren't in bed but were milling around the castle keep, drinking spiced wine and talking.

'Why is everyone still up?' Flora whispered as she and Gwen hung back in the shadows.

'It's because of the eclipse!' Gwen said. 'They must have decided to watch it.'

Flora bit her lip anxiously. 'If everyone's been outside watching the eclipse, Mother's *bound* to have noticed we've been missing.'

'Flora! Guinevere!' The swung round as they

heard Lady Matilda's voice. She was heading towards them. They both froze. 'Now, have you had something to eat and drink?' she said.

The girls looked at each other. Weren't they going to be told off?

'Well?' Lady Matilda said impatiently.

'Um . . . no, Mother,' said Flora slowly.

'Then go and help yourselves,' Lady Matilda replied. 'Wasn't the eclipse wonderful?'

'Yes . . . wonderful,' echoed Gwen, as her aunt smiled and glided away to speak to one of her ladies-in-waiting.

'She hadn't realised we were missing,' said Flora in surprise.

'Nineve must have been right,' Gwen whispered. 'Merlin did cast a spell so that nobody noticed we were missing!' She sent a silent thank you to Merlin in her head. It would have been awful to get back and find everyone looking for them. After all their hard work saving Avalon, they could have ended the night in lots of trouble.

'Let's get some food,' said Flora, looking towards the big banqueting table that had been set out in the keep.

They headed over. There were all sorts of delicious things to eat – warm cinnamon rolls, slices of meat studded with cloves and thick slices of apple pie.

'I'm still full from all the food we had with Nineve and the Spell Sisters,' Gwen whispered, rubbing her tummy. Still, she and Flora ate a little bit of food so nobody got suspicious, each of them stifling yawns. They were so tired. The day seemed to have gone on forever!

At last, people started to drift inside and the servants began to clear the food away. Gwen and

Flora retreated to their chamber.

'I'm so sleepy,' Flora said, flopping down on to her bed.

Gwen nodded, feeling exhaustion roll over her. Her bed looked very inviting.

Yawning, they changed into their nightclothes and fell into their soft beds. Within minutes they were both fast asleep.

It seemed only a few moments before the morning light was once again streaming through the windows, and the castle was ringing with the sound of voices. Gwen and Flora had to drag themselves out of their beds, but as soon as they were up they were swept along with the wedding preparations.

As bridesmaids, they had to help Cousin

Bethany dress and do her hair. Then there were flowers to carry to the chapel and decorations to put up in the Great Hall where the wedding breakfast would be served after the ceremony. When Bethany was ready, Gwen and Flora changed into their pale blue bridesmaid dresses. Flora tied her hair in neat braids trimmed with pale blue ribbons and put on the new bracelet that Nineve had given her. 'It matches my dress perfectly!' she said in delight.

Gwen was tugging a comb through her tangles. She seemed to have half the forest in her hair after the night before. She could never understand how Flora managed to make herself look so neat and perfect.

'Here, I'll help,' said Flora. 'You have to have your hair nice and tidy today.'

Gwen refused to have any ribbons put in,

but Flora did persuade her to hold her hair back from her face with a simple silver hairband that matched her pendant.

'There! You look lovely!' she declared.

Gwen pulled a face at herself in the looking glass. She didn't think she looked that lovely at all. She much preferred her old green day dress to the richly embroidered pale blue bridesmaid's dress and her old leather outdoor shoes to her soft kid skin boots!

Still, at least they were ready for the wedding. Giving her bow and arrows a last longing look, Gwen followed Flora down the stairs.

✦ ✦ ✦

The wedding was a great success – Bethany and Guy said their wedding vows perfectly and the chapel looked a very different place from the night before now it was decorated with flowers and filled with happy people. Gwen could hardly believe it was the scene of their confrontation with Morgana. She smiled as she walked out behind Bethany and Guy. The local villagers threw handfuls of rose petals over them all when outside the chapel.

✦ ✦ ✦

As people congratulated Bethany, Gwen stepped to one side and watched everyone milling around. Flora was talking to a cousin of Guy's. He was about fifteen, and very good looking. Flora was playing with her bracelet and smiling at him, her cheeks pink. Gwen chuckled to herself. It wouldn't be just Flora doing the teasing from now on!

Everyone had come to celebrate with the happy couple, and Gwen was delighted when she saw her mother, father and little sister Eleanor among those who had travelled from afar for the wedding. After the ceremony she rushed over to them and gave them a big hug hello. It had been so long since she'd seen them, and she couldn't wait to spend time with them today.

While her parents were talking with her Aunt Matilda and Uncle Richard, Gwen caught a hint of movement in the trees. She wandered closer to take a better look, peering through the tree trunks she gasped. There, standing in the sun-dappled shadows, were all eight of the Spell Sisters, with Moonlight! Moonlight whickered softly and the sisters waved.

Gwen waved back, grinning widely.

'Who are they?'

She spun round.

Arthur was standing behind her, looking curiously at the eight beautiful sisters and the white stallion. 'I've never seen them before,' he said, looking at Gwen curiously.

She hesitated. What could she say? 'It's . . .
um . . . Well . . . you know that secret I told you

about? They're part of it.'

'Oh.' Arthur looked at the group in the woods. 'It looks like an exciting secret.'

'Oh it is!' said Gwen with an apologetic smile. She longed to tell him about everything that had happened – about the drama and the danger, the spells and the magic. 'I really wish I could tell you all about it.'

'So, is this secret the reason why you and Flora keep going off into the woods?'

She nodded.

'Have you been in any danger?' he asked in concern.

'Well, yes!' she said, her eyes alight. 'But it was amazing!'

Arthur studied her happy face. 'You're really not like most girls, are you, Gwen?'

She rolled her eyes. 'No. Aunt Matilda is

always telling me I should be more ladylike.'

'Well, I'm glad you're not,' Arthur said. 'I like you as you are.'

For a moment Gwen felt unusually lost for words. A blush spread across the top of her cheekbones and she looked down.

Arthur cleared his throat. 'Hey, it looks like everyone's heading back to the castle now for the meal,' he said, glancing over his shoulder. 'We should probably go too.'

Gwen nodded and they fell into step, walking through the trees. Gwen glanced behind her and saw that the sisters and Moonlight had disappeared. She wondered when she would see them again. She touched her pendant and remembered Nineve's words: *your adventures are not over, Guinevere. I can promise you that.*

Good, Gwen thought fiercely. *I never want*

my adventures to be over.

She nudged Arthur. 'Race you to the castle.'

'You'll never beat me,' he scoffed.

'Oh really?' Gwen said, her green eyes challenging. 'Let's see. Last one there's a dung beetle!' She set off at top speed before Arthur could even draw a breath.

'Hey, wait!' he spluttered. 'Gwen!'

She raced on, jumping over tree roots and brambles, her laughter floating back through the trees.

In a Forest Clearing

The sunlight filtered through the trees and fell on the enormous hollowed-out oak tree that was Morgana's lair. She stood outside the entrance, her long hair wild, and her pale face full of rage. She had been defeated. Avalon was back in the power of the eight Spell Sisters.

'No!' she spat. Her hands clenched and unclenched. How could this have happened?

A leaf swirled down from the sky and she shot a ball of green fire at it, making it explode in a shower of sparks.

She scowled. Her plans had come to nothing and it was all the fault of those two girls. One day, she would make them pay.

'Oh yes,' she hissed, glaring at the sky. 'One day, I shall make them very sorry indeed!'

Swinging round, she stomped furiously into her lair.

HAVE YOU READ ALL OF GWEN
AND FLORA'S ADVENTURES?

DON'T MISS THE OTHER BOOKS
IN THE ✦Spell✦ SERIES!
Sisters

Find out how Gwen and Flora's
quest began in Sophia The Flame Sister...
Read on for a special extract...

The two girls headed deeper into the forest. Flora looked around nervously. 'I don't really like going this deep into the trees,' she said after a while. 'I always think there might be things watching me from the shadows.'

Gwen pretended to hide behind a tree and jumped out at her. 'What – you mean like monsters?' she grinned.

Flora pushed her playfully. 'No, but you know what people say. We've both heard the tales.' She shivered. 'The storytellers always say that the forest is a place where magical things happen. There could be dragons or enchanters or strange spirits! Maybe… maybe we should go home.'

'But I want to go on to the Lake,' Gwen argued.

'Do we really have to?'

'Yes!' Gwen insisted, linking arms with Flora. 'Look, I come into the forest lots, and nothing has ever happened to me.'

Flora let Gwen lead her further into the trees. 'I just wish it wasn't so quiet,' she said, her blue eyes darting around. 'Doesn't it feel strange to you, Gwen?'

Gwen paused for a moment. In her eagerness to get to the Lake, she hadn't noticed it, but now she had to admit that Flora was right. It was getting quieter and quieter as they headed closer to the Lake. There were no birds singing, no faint cracking of twigs as an animal passed by, and the trees' leaves were not golden and red here – they were brown and dull. A shiver ran across Gwen's skin.

'Let's go back,' said Flora, stopping suddenly. 'I don't like this.'

'No!' Gwen didn't know why, but she was suddenly filled with an urge to get to the Lake. It wasn't far away. Pulling away from Flora, she broke into a run, feeling like the Lake was somehow calling to her through the trees. She couldn't turn back now!

'Wait, Gwen!'

Gwen ignored her cousin. She jumped over gnarled roots, scrambled past thick bushes and finally pushed her way out between the trunks of the trees that surrounded the Lake. Her heart was pounding, but to her relief the Lake looked just as it usually did. The glittering water shone and a feeling of peace and quiet hung in the air.

Gwen let out a breath. For one dreadful moment she had thought that she was going to see something different – that somehow the Lake would have changed in some horrible way.

Flora appeared through the trees, a twig caught in her neat hair, a smudge on her cheek.

'It's just like it always is…' Gwen's voice trailed off as she spoke. No matter what she'd felt before, she was here now and she was happy to just enjoy the Lake.

Kicking off her boots, she reached under her dress and wriggled out of her woollen tights. Then, with her bare feet sinking into the short cold grass, she ran down the bank to the edge of the Lake. Holding up her skirt, she gasped as the icy water covered her toes.

Flora followed her more cautiously, edging down the bank and going over to sit on a cluster of rocks at the side of the Lake. But, just as she was about to settle herself down, Flora let out a surprised cry. 'There's something here, Gwen, look! A silver chain!'

Gwen glanced back briefly and saw Flora crouching beside one of the rocks. 'It's probably just some lady's necklace that a magpie stole and dropped,' Gwen called over her shoulder, taking a step deeper into the water.

'It doesn't look like it's been dropped,' said Flora. 'It looks as if it's caught in the rock.'

Gwen shrugged. The Lake was so clear she could see straight down to the pebbles on the bottom. She moved her toes, making the water swirl.

'Come and see, Gwen!' Flora insisted. 'It's really strange.'

With a sigh, Gwen went over. Flora was pulling at the chain but it wouldn't budge. The rock's surface was as smooth as a mirror, and the silver chain seemed to be almost growing out of the centre of it. Gwen felt a flicker of surprise. She'd expected there to be a crack or something that the chain was caught in, but there wasn't. Flora was right – it looked like part of the chain was actually inside the rock.

'It's stuck fast!' said Flora, giving it another tug.

'Here, let me have a go!' Gwen took the chain. As her fingers closed around the metal she could have sworn she felt a strange tingle run through her hands and up her arms. She gave a pull. With a faint clink and clatter, the chain slid easily out of the rock, sending Gwen staggering back with a surprised cry.

For a moment, Gwen stood in the water, staring at the necklace in her hands. A large blue pendant dangled from it.

'How did you do that?' Flora exclaimed. 'I pulled as hard as I could and it wouldn't move.'

Gwen was just as astonished. She stared down at the necklace. 'I… I don't know.' The large blue pendant seemed to glow and shine. She'd never seen anything like it. Holding it up, Gwen stared at it, her eyes wide with wonder. As she watched, the pendant suddenly seemed to twist and turn as if it had a life of its own.

Gwen jumped and dropped the necklace – but instead of it falling to the ground, it floated up into the air as if carried by invisible hands.

Flora shrieked.

Gwen's mouth fell open. For once, she was lost for words.

The pendant twirled around in the air, coming closer and closer to Gwen. It dangled in front of her face and suddenly she was filled with the urge to touch it. She reached out.

'No, Gwen, don't!' gasped Flora.

But it was too late. As Gwen's trembling fingers touched the glowing stone, there was a

bright silver flash. Gwen blinked, and then heard a faint click like a clasp shutting. She felt a heaviness around her neck, and as she looked down a startled exclamation burst from her lips. The beautiful necklace had fastened itself around her neck!

Magic! Her thoughts whirled. *It's magic!*

Gwen's fingers closed around the pendant. She couldn't explain it, but it somehow felt like it had been waiting for her – that it *belonged* to her.

'What's happening?' breathed Flora, her eyes wide.

A bright light seemed to shine out over a spot in the Lake. 'Look!' Gwen exclaimed.

They both stared as the light grew brighter and brighter, and then the waters parted. To their amazement, a beautiful young woman rose up to the surface.

Gwen stared. What was happening? Was this woman a water nymph – a spirit of the water? Or maybe she was a goddess or a sorceress? As Flora had said, Gwen *had* heard the storytellers who came to the castle telling tales of magical beings who lived throughout the land. Could it really be true?

'I... I don't like this!' Flora stammered, backing away.

Gwen's heart was banging against her ribs, but she was rooted to the spot. She bravely faced the woman and called out: 'Who are you?'

'My name is Nineve.' The woman's voice was low and musical. Her long chestnut-brown hair swept all the way down to her feet, held back from her face by a sparkling pearl headband. Her dress shimmered with different shades of green and blue all the way down to her bare feet.

As the girls watched, she began to float across
the surface of the water towards them...

MAKE YOUR OWN WIND VANE

Follow the instructions below and make your own
wind vane to measure and track the direction of
the wind in your garden – who knows, maybe
it's being created by Chloe's magical powers!

What you'll need:

+ A plastic ice-cream container lid
  (or an old food container lid)

+ Scissors or a craft knife   + A pin

+ A marker or felt-tip pen   + Glue

+ A wooden skewer   + Blue Tack

+ A drinking straw

*Remember to
always be careful when
you're working with
scissors and glue or
ask a grown-up to
help you.*

TOP TIPS

+ *Why not paint your wind vane
a bright colour or colours to add some
sparkle to your garden?*

+ *Your wind vane will also tell you
just how fast the wind is going,
the quicker the spin, the faster
the wind.*

HOW TO MAKE YOUR
WIND VANE:

1. Draw a triangle on to the ice-cream container lid with the marker and cut it out. Repeat the process but this time draw and cut out a rectangle. Write the letter "S" on the triangle and "N" on the rectangle.

2. Cut a slit in both ends of your straw. Slide the triangle (on a flat edge) on one end so that it looks like an arrowhead. Then slide the rectangle on the other end. Glue into place.

3. Push the pin through the exact middle of the straw and then use the pin to secure the straw to the flat end of the skewer.

4. Find somewhere in your garden or on a window sill to secure the wind vane to, use the blue tack to hold it in place. Wait for the wind to blow and note which way your vane is pointing – "S" for south or "N" for North.

VISIT WWW.SPELLSISTERS.CO.UK AND

Plus lots of other enchanted extras!

Spell Sisters news

Explore Avalon

More about Gwen and Flora's quest

Spell Sister profiles

Activity sheets

Wallpapers

Your chance to get in touch with us

ENTER THE MAGICAL WORLD OF AVALON!

www.spellsisters.co.uk

SIMON AND SCHUSTER